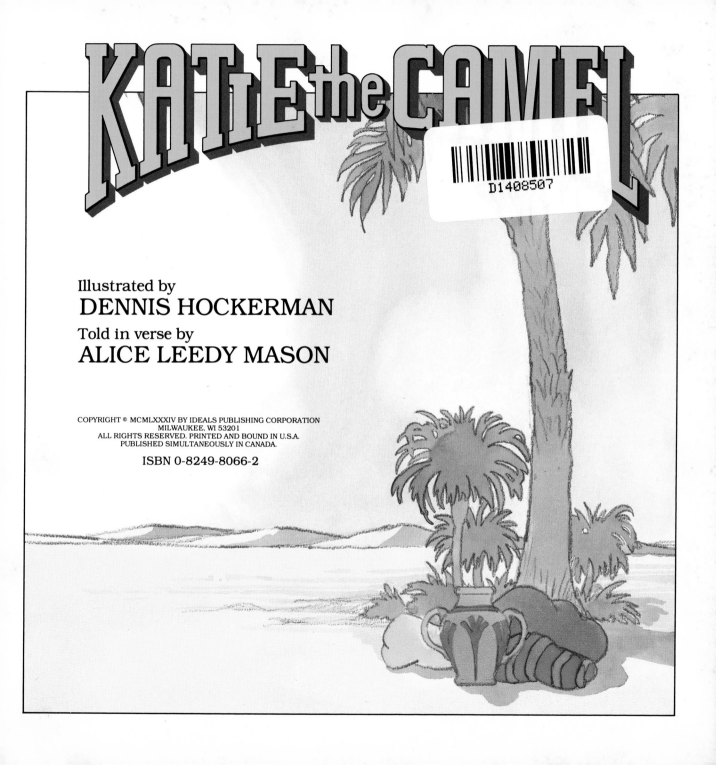

KATiE the CAMEL

Illustrated by
DENNIS HOCKERMAN
Told in verse by
ALICE LEEDY MASON

ISBN 0-8249-8066-2

The camels were ready to start a new journey;
This was young Katie's first trip.
 Because she was new
 And a bit nervous too,
Leader Caspar helped out with a tip.

Drink plenty of water," kind Caspar advised.
"We'll go west — stay close and you'll see.
 The oasis is grand,
 Like mirages in sand,
With the sweetest of dates on each tree!"

Mirages in sand —
Katie knew about those.
To see one would be lots of fun.
Other camels had told
Of this mystery of old —
Of oases that vanished in sun.

Mile after mile — and Katie grew tired.
Strong winds blew the sand and made her eyes weep.
  She couldn't recall
  Her directions at all,
So she crouched on the ground and fell fast asleep.

When she opened her eyes the desert had changed.
The sand storm was over, the caravan gone.
   Wind had shifted the sand
   To a smooth trackless land.
There was no one to tell her which way to go on.

Katie tried very hard to remember directions.
She knew that the caravan moved toward the west.
   Since the sun went its way
   Traveling west every day,
To follow the sun seemed the plan that was best.

From sand dune to sand dune,
  each step grew harder.
Katie struggled to hold back a tear.
  She longed to hear words
  And see camels in herds,
And she silently prayed
  the sweet dates would appear.

Soon she stood at the top
of the highest sand dune.
Far in the distance an oasis appeared.
Green trees, pool of blue,
Camel caravan too;
Only a mirage was that lovely, she feared.

Katie stopped for a moment, half afraid to go on.
The vision was lovely — was it one she could trust?
She was turning away
When she heard Caspar say,
"It's us Katie! And dates! Come on out of the dust!"

When your goal seems far away,
Trying hard can save the day.